Ascension Stage: Feauvium 76b5

By Mark F Kalita

To connect with the author, please visit:
www.KALITA.com

To continue with the story, please visit:
www.AscensionStage.com

The Council of Realms, in protecting the Octaves, has approved this account of experience within ONE for the benefit of the Intelligent Infinity.

Feauvium 76b5
5th Octave of Darkness

Chapter 1

With the downlight glow, the children get no sleep within their cages. The wire mesh above them allows the constant dripping of rain through a weather worn roof.

Dnogn opens the door as they all huddle to the back corner of their cages in a fleeting attempt to find shelter.

Dnogn walks a few steps into the room and pauses, looking at the dozens of cages crammed with his food. He smiles and begins to walk to a cage in the corner of the barn.

He bends down and opens the door to the cage.

As Dnogn reaches in to grab a child, they all try to scratch and claw at his arm. One small hand, with razor sharp nails, connects with it's target and slices through Dnogn's thick, gray skin.

Pulling his arm back, and out of the cage, Dnogn squeals, "Aayyaa, you little ones mustn't be so cross at me. You are my fodder tonight. Come, so Dnogn eats."

With that, Dnogn stands, closing the cage door. He picks up one side of the cage and shakes it. The children fall to the back of the cage, toppling on each other. Dnogn shakes it again, and again, until the little beasts are quelled.

Dnogn places the cage back on the floor of the dusky barn. He bends down and looks in. The small ones are stunned and paralyzed momentarily.

He opens the cage door and reaches in again, grabs one by the foot, pulls it out and quickly shuts the cage door before any other little ones react.

As he pulls the child out, it comes to it's senses and starts screaming and flailing around.

"Calm down, little one," Dnogn speaks. "this will be over shortly, for you."

In front of the cage, Dnogn smiles as his free hand wraps around the tiny head of his prize. With the other children in the cages watching, he twists the head, snapping the neck of the child.

In shock, the children begin to howl in disgust and fear. Some are heard crying. Others are just gasping, unable to form words.

"You should be so lucky," Dnogn speaks to them, holding the lifeless body of the child above him. "This one is free of the misery of this day. Now, with help from the great Dnogn, it is one step closer to the reckoning."

Dnogn drops his arm with the limp child in it.

He turns and walks out of the barn as the children look at him in horror.

Chapter 2

Dnogn exits the Holding Barn, dragging the lifeless victim for his eventide meal by his side. The dull glow of the dying sun barely lights his path. The thick soles of his feet walk swiftly across the rocky terrain.

Dnogn lifts his head, looking in the direction of Abneof who is sitting beside the fire pit. A bit smaller than Dnogn, Abneof is none the less fierce. Hairless gray skin covers a lean muscular build.

Feauviums are not known for their intelligence. They are a race of survivalists. The harsh environment of Feauvium 76b5 is one of the darkest in the entire Council of Realms. It is here that Angels learn the greatest lessons of Darkness.

As Dnogn walks up to the fire pit, he gets agitated that Abneof has not lit the fire. He begins to walk faster towards Abneof.

As he approaches, Dnogn grunts loudly and startles Abneof.

"Hold the little one," Dnogn grunts, handing the child to Abneof. "Dnogn gotta get the fire burnin hot. blacken nears and Crackel be huntin tonight."

"Yah, get it burnin," Abneof concurs as he grabs the dead child from Dnogn,

"What have you been doin, Abneof?", Dnogn questions. "We don't have enough bones for the fire."

"I sit. I think," Abneof responds.

"You? You think? Hahaha," Dnogn laughs at his sub-alpha. "You don't think, you do. Dnogns survive. Thinking dies."

"Get burnin goin," Abneof responds. "Then, I go to Crush House and get more bones. I'm hungry."

"You always hungry," Dnogn responds angrily.

As Abneof sits with the child in his lap, drooling, Dnogn starts throwing the bones into the pit. He grabs a femur and pauses, looking at it closely. He puts it to his mouth and scrapes off a bit of flesh then throws the bone into the pile.

"Put the little one down," Dnogn instructs Abneof. "Let's douse the bones."

Dnogn walks to the edge of the fire pit and begins to urinate on the bones. Abneof puts down the child and stands. He joins Dnogn next to the fire pit and also begins to urinate.

The strong smell of ammonia and gases rise in the air as the two empty their bladders on the pit.

"Stand back," Dnogn instructs Abneof as he finishes urinating.

Dnogn turns around and grabs two sharpened stones from the side of the pit. He stands over the bones. With a great force, he strikes the two stones together creating sparks that fly into the pit. Immediately, the rising gases catch the sparks and ignite the bones below. The resulting fire explodes.

Dnogn jumps back quickly so he isn't burned.

"Now, go," Dnogn instructs Abneof who is holding tight to the child. "No worry. I won't eat before you return. And, be careful of the Crackel. You be a tasty morsel to them beasts."

Abneof stands and hesitates as he hands Dnogn the child, asking, "You no eat before I return?"

"Go, quickly," Dnogn replies. "I am hungry. You hurry there might be scraps left. GO!"

Abneof growls, grimacing at Dnogn as he turns and runs.

Dnogn laughs as he sits down, patting the young child on the head as he places it in his lap.

Chapter 3

Panting, Abneof stops running for a moment with the Crush House just on the horizon. Fearfully, he looks around the barren landscape for Crackel. Seeing none, he takes a deep breath and moves forward.

Walking quickly, Abneof steadily picks up his pace until he is running again. Straining through his hunger, but determined to make it to the Crush House, his hard footfalls are not affected by the sharp rocks he is sailing across.

Feauviums have evolved over many thousands of years, adapting to the harsh environment of this planet. As many other realms within the ONE, Fauvium began as an unspoiled realm, primitive and untouched by the hands of those who believed it was theirs to own.

Once the Council of Realms determined, through the Intelligent Infinity, that Feauvium was to enter the Ascension Stage, the terra-forming began and the advancement through the Octaves was scheduled.

Not unlike other realms, Feauvium was populated with 3rd Octave Angels initially. Then, through the lessons of Service to Others and Service to Self, Feauvium went from Light to Dark after the Angels destroyed the planet.

Now, a Realm within the 5th Octave of Darkness, Feauvium 76b5 is one of the most sought after realms for Angels who wish to experience the Darkness of ONE.

Abneof and Dnogn are two of the Dark Angels who chose to enter this realm. Now, nearing the eventuality of their full experience of Darkness, they are top among the Dark Angels within this realm.

Yet, their struggle is constant as they battle hunger, the environment and Crackel- named for the sound they make as they bite down on Feauviums.

Nearing the Crush House, Abneof smells the sweet odor of flesh being ripped from the bones of those too old to be eaten fresh. The Crush House is the factory where those children older than 7 years old are sent to be ground as food for the young children. Here, the flesh is separated from the bones and fermented into a gruel that is easily digested by the young ones.

Outside of the Crush House, the bones of the children are in piles so the owners can gather them for fuel. For each Crush House that is in Feauvium, there are approximately a dozen owners of children who contribute to the operation. Daily, the owners, or their helpers, gather the gruel and bones to continue their operation. Abneof is the sub-alpha of Dnogn, an owner.

As Abneof approaches the Crush House, a voice calls from inside, "Who comes?"

Abneof stops, bows as he outstretches his arms, and states, "Abneof, from the farm of Dnogn. I come to collect bones."

"It's late, Abneof," the voice yells, chuckling. "Good luck. You may proceed."

Abneof looks around and runs toward the bones.

Anxious, and not looking where he is going, Abneof trips over a rock and flies head first into the pile, burying himself in the bones. Struggling to get out, his head peaks through the pile in time to see a pack of Crackel on the horizon.

Holding his breath and not moving, he is hoping that the sentry in the Crush House sends repellent towards the pack. While he doesn't want to get caught in the spray, Abneof doesn't want to become food for the pack either.

Suddenly, the alarm sounds and the perimeter is sprayed with repellent.

Abneof sinks beneath the bones to limit his exposure. Safely under the cover of bones, he stays there until the siren and repellent ceases.

Abeneof jumps out, gathers as many bones as he can carry and runs off into the night, covered in the urine and feces of the processed children.

At least, he thinks to himself, the Crackel won't want to gobble him up so quickly.

Chapter 4

Dnogn sits by the fire, petting the head of the dead child in his lap, staring into the fire. He hears growls just outside the perimeter of the fire circle and stands looking in the direction of the growl. Not seeing anything, he sits back down.

"Ah, little one, you don't know how lucky you are to be made into food. I cannot wait for my final days so I can get closer to my reckoning," Dnogn speaks to the dead child. "I have been here so long and if I wasn't so close to my reckoning, I would end it all now."

Sitting, petting, Dnogn is pulling genetic emotions from deep within himself. As the Feauviums are a race of owner predators, feelings of compassion are typically non-existent. For a Feauvium, survival of the fittest is the prime directive of life.

Suddenly, there are screams and howls from the Holding Barn. Dnogn stands quickly and turns towards the barn. The screams continue as Dnogn begins to get agitated.

"STOP," Dnogn yells.

The screaming and howling continues.

Dnogn looks in the direction that Abneof ran then turns back to the Holding Barn. He starts to grumble and pace. He pounds his feet on the ground as he walks violently around the fire.

"NO, NO," Dnogn exclaims. "STOP!"

Now getting angry, Dnogn strains to look into the darkened environment around him. Sensing nothing, he begins to run to the Holding Barn, carrying the dead child under his arm.

As he approaches, the screaming and howling gets louder. Emanating from within the Holding Barn, the children in cages are throwing a fit for some reason. Dnogn must figure out what is happening to his prized possessions before he looses his entire crop.

Dnogn gets to the door of the barn and throws it open. Shocked, the children in cages stop their screaming and howling momentarily, looking in the direction of Dnogn.

"NO NOISE," Dnogn yells. "SLEEP, YOUNGUNS!"

For a moment, the caged children are quiet. Then, all at once and in unison, they begin yelling, screaming and violently shaking their cages.

"AAAYYYAAAYYYYY," Dnogn screams while holding the dead child he has been carrying above his head. "SEE. DO YOU ALL WANT TO BE LIKE THIS?"

The entire barn is quiet as Dnogn stands before the cages. He is holding the limp, dead child above his head. Slowly, he lowers it and grabs a dead hand with his free hand. Slipping the fingers of the child into his mouth, rows of teeth bite down and a loud 'CRUNCH' echoes through the silence of the barn.

The children in the cages, gasp and climb down from the walls and ceilings of their cages.

Dnogn continues to crunch the fingers of the child with every bite.

One of the caged children rushes to the front of his cage and starts screaming and howling at Dnogn.

Dnogn pounds his feet on the ground, screams at the unruly child and takes another bite of finger, sounding a loud 'CRUNCH' in his direction.

The child begins to whimper, becoming submissive again and returns to the back of his cage with the other children, awaiting their destiny on Feauvium.

Chapter 5

"Dnogn, Dnogn," Abneof calls into the darkness, now back at the fire pit with an arm full of bones. "Dnogn, where are you?"

"I'm here," Dnogn responds walking back from the Holding Barn. "Those children were acting up again. I had to go quiet them down."

"I got more bones," Abneof exclaims. "I'm hungry. Let's eat the little one now."

"Settle," Dnogn says. "Throw some more bones on the fire and sit."

Abneof submits to Dnogn and throws bones onto the fire. Dnogn sits on his boulder. Abneof sits next to him.

Dnogn rips the arm off the child with the chewed fingers and gives it to Abneof.

"What?", Abneof exclaims. "You already ate the tender fingers. Gimme that one."

"NO," Dnogn yells. "These are MY children. You are mine too. EAT!"

Abneof lowers his head in submission. He opens his mouth, stuffing the entire hand in, biting it off at the wrist. With every bite, rows of teeth grind the soft bones with an eerie crunch. Abneof smiles.

Meanwhile, Dnogn rips off the other arm of the child and takes his time, eating one tender finger after another.

"Ahhh, this child is yummy," Abneof states. "Which brood grew this one?"

"Good question, subbie," Dnogn retorts. "I think it was young Xechia. She is ready to make another. I will take her tonight."

"Me too," Abneof adds. "Gotta be sure she makes more tasty treats like this."

Dnogn looks at Abneof as he bites the hand off the child, and laughs, "Yes, ha ha ha, gotta get her good and full of tasty treats."

Chapter 6

Feauvium was stripped of resources thousands of years ago. The only animals left are the Crackel. There are no plants or trees. The star at the center of the solar system has been dying for longer than anyone can remember.

Dnogn is not a name, it is the leader of this particular tribe of Feauviums. This is the Dnogn clan. It is one of the largest clans in all of Feauvium.

There is a Brood House in the compound of Dnogn. In the Brood House, the girls and women live out their lives.

From birth, the girls are separated from the boys. The boys live in the Holding Barn. The girls live with the women in the Brood House.

The function of the women in Feauvium is pleasure for the alpha male and producing children for food and fuel. If they can not bear children, they are sent to the Crush House to be made into fodder.

In return, they are protected and fed.

It is the only life they know.

It is the only way to survive on this dark planet.

The alternative is to wander the barren landscape of Feauvium, be eaten by Crackel or be taken by another clan who may, or may not, treat them as well as Dnogn does.

The only thing they have is each other – and Dnogn.

Tonight, as every night in Feauvium, the women are preparing for their Dnogn to come and seed them. It is their nightly ritual. Not only do the eligible women prepare to be seeded by Dnogn, the young girls are hidden and protected by the older women.

Only Abneof knows the real status of the women and girls in the Brood House. As he is the sub-alpha of Dnogn, Abneof is in charge of feeding the women and girls. He also keeps their numbers lean by taking the useless women to the Crush House.

And, occasionally, he partakes in a young girl when he is hungry.

Chapter 7

The door to the Brood House swings open and Dnogn walks in, followed by Abneof. Dnogn stops cold in his tracks, just a couple of steps inside the door. Abneof, looking down, almost runs into him.

The dozens of available women of the brood who are in the large entry room look up to see Dnogn in the doorway. They straighten up and smile wicked smiles hoping that they would be next to carry Dnogn's seed.

"I'm here my brood," Dnogn announces. "Line up my pretties and let me see who wants Dnogn seed tonight."

The women quickly scurry to the front of the room and stand at attention before Dnogn.

Dnogn paces back and forth in front of the line inspecting his treasures. One by one, he touches, gropes and sniffs each woman.

Abneof still stands in place, head down and waiting for instruction from Dnogn.

"Abneof," Dnogn loudly calls from the end of the room. "I do not see young Xechia. Find her."

"Yes, Dnogn," Abneof states as he scurries off into another room.

Dnogn stands, tapping his right foot anxiously on the ground.

"Abneof," Dnogn screams. "NOW!"

Suddenly, a back door quickly swings open and Abneof rushes through it, dragging Xechia by the arm. He drags her to the front of the room and throws her before Dnogn. Xechia lands on her knees and stays down, bowing to Dnogn. Abneof takes his position behind Dnogn.

"Why were you hiding from me, Xechia?," Dnogn asks. "Do you refuse to take my seed, woman?"

Xechia looks up at Dnogn and scowls, "I refuse nothing. I'm yours, so take me like an animal, Dnogn."

Dnogn growls.

He looks up from Xechia at the other women in the room and starts to belly laugh, "Ha ha ha. My women, you could learn something from this one. She has spirit. Her children are tasty. She knows she will have my seed tonight and plays games with Dnogn."

Dnogn reaches down and grabs Xechia by the arm, standing her next to him. He reaches around, grabs Abneof by the neck and pushes him down in front of him. Abneof falls to his knees.

"I am Dnogn," Dnogn states standing tall before his brood. "You are mine. Tonight I give you my seed. I give you the seed of my sub-alpha. Drain us so that we might eat and survive in this dark land."

"Women of my brood, take this weak man. I want to watch as you consume him. I want to watch as he spills his seed so I can eat the little ones you carry."

As Dnogn, speaks, the crowd of women start chanting and jeering.

"NOW," Dnogn commands.

With his instructions, the horde of women surround Abneof. As the women of Feauvium are much smaller than the men, it takes seven of them to pick him up to carry him to the back of the room.

As they take Abneof, Dnogn turns to Xechia, grabs her by the arm and says, "I had a tasty little boy of yours tonight for meal. I want more. Come, take my seed young Xechia."

Dnogn pulls her to the opposite side of the room from where Abneof was taken. Upon reaching his bed, he throws Xechia on top of it. He climbs onto his bed and Xechia scowls at him.

Dnogn lays down on his bed.

Xechia climbs on top of him, preparing to take his seed.

Once on top, she slaps Dnogn hard across the face, breaking his skin with her finger nails.

Dnogn grabs her neck and chokes her, now pressing deep inside of her.

Chapter 8

Dnogn wakes to the howling of women. He sits up suddenly and shakes his head to clear his thoughts. He looks around the room to see where the noise came from. Across the room, there are three women still trying to drain the seed from Abneof.

Abneof is being held down as one of the women is on top of him gyrating and howling.

"ENOUGH," Dnogn exclaims as he jumps up from his bed. "I need Abneof to work now. Night is done. Day is now. Women get on with your chores."

The women scatter.

Abneof is laying on the makeshift bed, barely moving.

"Up now, Abneof," Dnogn orders. "Playtime is done. Work is NOW!"

Dnogn grabs Abneof by a foot and hurls him across the room. Abneof gains his composure quickly, squats and scowls at Dnogn, showing his teeth.

"NO," Dnogn exclaims as he runs to confront Abneof who is visually in a state of defiance.

Dnogn stands tall above Abneof, showing his superiority.

Abneof bows his head and whimpers in submission.

"That's better, you fool," Dnogn states. "Now, get up. You feed boys. You go to Crush House today."

"Yes, Dnogn," Abneof says. "I am sorry, Dnogn. Please forgive me. The women used Abneof too much. My mind was still in flesh."

"Ha ha ha," Dnogn chuckles. "Too much flesh. Should've got sleep. You better work today. I best not find you slackin'."

"No, Dnogn," Abneof concurs. "No slackin'. I feed boys gruel. I feed women gruel. I take old boys and old women to Crush House. I get bones and gruel for Dnogn."

"Yes, Abneof," Dnogn pats Abneof on the head. "That's a good sub-alpha boy. You do that and maybe Dnogn give Abneof more flesh tonight. NOW GO!"

Abneof, scared at Dnogn's last outburst, backs up quickly and makes his way out of the Brood House.

"Women," Dnogn yells as he turns, walking to the back of the Brood House. "Dnogn hungry. I want tender little girl for breakfast. Here I come."

Chapter 9

Abneof opens the door to the Holding Barn and the boys start howling and jumping around in their cages. It's morning and Abneof is late for their feeding.

"It's ok little ones," Abneof speaks. "I've got your gruel, just calm down children. You'll eat shortly."

Abneof goes into the corner where the barrel of gruel is located. He grabs a scoop and a bucket. He begins to scoop the gruel into the bucket.

"Most of you will never know the next year," Abneof begins to talk softly as the boys begin to calm down. "One of you might take my place one day. Abneof is getting tired of Dnogn."

The boys screech like they know what he is saying.

"I know, I know," Abneof turns towards the boys in the cages. "You don't like Dnogn. He just comes in to take the boys. Abneof cares for boys."

Abneof walks to each cage, fills a bowl in front of it and opens the cage, placing the bowl in the cage with the boys. Once inside, the boys circle the bowls and lap up the gruel. After Abneof gets to the last cage, he goes back to the first and pours gruel over the cage, aiming for the bowl. He continues down the line for all the cages.

"There you go boys," Abneof consoles. "That should keep you for another day. Dnogn will be in shortly to take one of you out of this cruelty."

As the boys are finishing their gruel, Abneof takes an accounting of the boys. He is looking for the oldest and toughest boys to take to the Crush House. He will trade them for more gruel and bones.

"I'm going to take a couple of you for a walk today," Abneof starts talking as he is removes the bowls from the cages. "You will get to see this desolate planet at least once before you get closer to the reckoning."

Abneof goes from cage to cage, pulling the bowls out and closing the cage doors. The boys are quiet with full bellies. They timidly watch him as he goes about his work.

At one point, while Abneof has a cage open, he hears a sound and turns. He pulls the bowl out of the cage. In his tiredness, and being distracted, he forgets to lock the cage.

The boys, sitting at the rear of the cage, don't make a sound. They look at each other and grin.

Abneof finishes putting the bowls back.

He walks over to the wall, grabs a long chain and throws it over his shoulder. The chain has a number of hardened metal ankle cuffs. He walks back to the cages with the chain.

Abneof kneels in front of a cage, opens it, pulls an older boy out and locks the cage. The boy doesn't struggle. The gruel has a sedative-like affect. The boy is calm as Abneof places a cuff around his ankle.

Still holding the chain, Abneof walks to another cage and repeats the process with another older boy.

"I need one more boy today," Abneof thinks out loud. "I guess I will take you."

Abneof kneels in front of another cage and repeats the process, taking a third boy out and chaining him.

"That should do for today, boys," Abneof tell them. "I will be back tomorrow to feed you some more. Be nice to Dnogn. He isn't so bad. He just does what he has to do."

Abneof stops and looks around at the cages and shakes his head. He is tired and his energy is low. He walks with his head down towards the door.

He stops.

"I knew I was forgetting something," Abneof exclaims.

He walks over to the barrel of gruel, grabs a bucket and begins to fill it.

"Gotta get some treats for the women, too," Abneof tells the boys.

He turns and walks back towards the door.

"C'mon boys, let's walk."

Chapter 10

Abneof opens the door to the Brood House and pulsl the boys in. He wraps the chain around a hook next to the front door.

"Women," Abneof calls out, walking towards a table in the corner of the room. "I've got a bucket of gruel for you."

The two doors at the rear of the large room open. A couple of dozen women come out with bowls in hand. They line up orderly in front of the bucket. One by one they dip their bowl in, step aside and drink the gruel down.

After they are done with their first bowl of gruel, each woman gets back in line.

As the first woman to get a bowl of gruel reaches the bucket again, she dips her bowl back into the bucket to fill her bowl. This time, instead of drinking the bowl of gruel, she carefully walks it back through the door.

One by one, each of the women do the same thing.

"Make sure the little ones get there fill, too," Abneof instructs. "Take care of your sisters. We want them to grow up to make lots of babies so Dnogn gets lots more gruel and bones."

"See boys," Abneof turns to the three boys in chains, "if you were older, you could give your seed to these women. Too bad you will never know flesh like Abneof."

As the last of the women finish filling their bowl and walking into the back room, Abneof takes the bucket and sips the last drops of gruel from the bucket. He then walks the bucket next to the door and places it on the floor.

"Wait here boys," Abneof states as he pats one of the boys on the head. "I've got to find a couple of women. Then we take a walk to the Crush House."

Chapter 11

Dnogn walks into the Holding Barn and shuts the door behind him. The boys are quiet and subdued. He looks around at the cages and smiles. He turns and walks over to the barrel of gruel.

He looks inside, inspecting the contents. He sticks his finger in and tastes the concoction.

"Yuck," he states, shaking his finger off. "That gruel is nasty stuff. I prefer little ones."

Dnogn smiles and looks over the cages. He walks back and forth, examining the boys inside.

"Dnogn is hungry," he states as he points to a cage with a small boy in it. "I think I want you."

The boys are still full from the meal they had less than an hour ago.

Dnogn bends down and opens the cage. He reaches in. The boys whimper but do not fight back.

Dnogn grabs one little boy boy by the foot and begins to pull him out. The boy tugs on the wall of the cage, but Dnogn pulls hard.

"You just ate," Dnogn tells him. "I have to squeeze you to get that nasty gruel out. Don't fight me and this will be over soon."

Dnogn grabs the boy by his feet and holds him over the barrel. The boy is limp but still squirms a bit as Dnogn is holding him.

Dnogn wraps his hand around the boys mid section and squeezes hard, forcing the gruel into the barrel.

The boy chokes and gasps.

Dnogn then turns the boy over and holds him by the neck. He squeezes tight. As the boy dies, he empties his bowels into the corner of the Holding Barn.

The boys in the cages start to get agitated. They begin to howl and shake their cages.

"Calm down little ones," Dnogn speaks. "You are still alive, for the moment. Just lay there in your happy full belly feelings."

Dnogn walks to the corner of the barn and sits on an overturned barrel. He places the dead boy in his lap and grabs a hand. Placing the hand in his mouth, he bites down hard, ripping the hand off with a loud 'CRUNCH'.

The boys in the cages become more and more agitated with every crunching chew that Dnogn makes.

The boys in the cage that Abneof didn't lock look at each other and grin. They shake their heads in silent agreement and slowly make their way to the front of their cage.

Dnogn is busy eating the young boy in his lap. He is not paying attention to the cages.

The boys in the unlocked cage slowly open the door to their cage as the other boys are causing a raucous.

Silently, they exit their cage and spread out among the other cages, carefully unlocking them as Dnogn eats.

With a loud piercing scream, the boys simultaneously open their cages and run out.

Dnogn is shocked and spits out a mouthful of boy.

"STOP," Dnogn yells, standing and throwing the dead boy to the ground. "GET BACK IN YOUR CAGES."

Dnogn, barely able to finish his sentence, is attacked by the boys. They climb all over him, clawing and scratching him with their razor sharp nails. Unable to defend himself with so many boys, Dnogn falls to the ground.

As he falls, the boys run to the door and open it. Pushing and shoving, they make their way out the door and to freedom from Dnogn.

Dnogn, laying on the ground, barely having the strength to whisper, says, "You'll be back - if you're not already dead."

Chapter 12

The Dnogn boys stream out of the Holding Barn. They are now running across the barren landscape screaming and hollering as they make their way to freedom. Running blind, they scatter in all directions. For some, the light on the exterior is too much to handle and they have to stop and adjust their eyes to the dim morning sun.

The sharp rocks are tearing at their soft, unworn feet. Blood is littering the surrounding lands.

The Crackel sense the injuries as they raise their heads to smell the sweet scent of flesh.

Running now, in packs, the Crackel swiftly approach the Dnogn camp. They see the young boys running in the distance. They pick up their speed to head off the escaping boys.

While some are sitting, tending to their wounds, others see the approaching threat and seek shelter. Some are running back to the safety of the Holding Barn. Many are running to the hills in the distance.

As the Crackel come upon the horde of boys, they begin to scoop up the little ones with their giant mouths and crack them in two. The boys try to maneuver away from the hungry beasts to no avail. The Crackel's ravenous appetites are slowly being quenched with every Dnogn boy they eat.

Suddenly, they stop in their tracks and retreat.

Dnogn has gained his strength and is now running towards the Crackel, screaming and howling. Unafraid of the Crackel, Dnogn is waving sharpened bones in each hand. His noise and forcefulness frightens the Crackel as they run.

Stopping to catch his breath, Dnogn screams, "GO BACK BOYS. DNOGN PROTECTS YOU LITTLE ONES."

More fearful of Dnogn than the Crackel, the boys begin to head back to the Holding Barn.

Dnogn slowly walks back, following the many little ones who survived.

As Dnogn walks, he stops to pick up as many injured boys as he can. Holding onto his back and in his arms, Dnogn gives them strange love on the way back to the Holding Barn.

Dnogn pushes the door open and puts the boys that he is carrying on the ground. They scurry to their cages and go inside.

Dnogn takes his time locking all of the cages and counting what's left of his little ones.

Chapter 13

Abneof is walking up to the Crush House with the three boys and two women in chains to trade them for more gruel and bones. Still tired from his long night, and equally long walk through the harsh environment of Feauvium, he hopes that he can rest a bit before his long trek home to the Dnogn camp.

"We are almost to the Crush House," Abneof tells the Feauviums he has in tow. "Take in this last bit of your world, for tomorrow you will be closer to the reckoning."

Pulling the five in tow, Abneof knocks on the door to the Crush House.

"Who's a knockin'," a voice from inside calls.

"It's Abneof. From the clan of Dnogn."

The door opens and a large Feauvium peaks out.

"Abneof, so good to see you, again," the man chuckles. "Wasn't that you bone collectin' last night?"

"Yes," Abneof replies, lowering his head.

"I thought so," the man chuckles again. "You gotta good sprayin' of the juice last night. I bet the women liked you lots back at Dnogn."

Abneof picks up his head and hotly comments, "Yes, thank you for that! It kept the Crackel off of me for the run back."

"Ha ha ha, I bet it did," the man laughs. "What you got for the Crush House today from clan Dnogn?"

"I've got three little ones and two useless women for gruel and bones today," Abneof responds.

"Not very good specimens," the man adds. "But, you can have as much gruel and bones as you can carry. As matter of fact, you can take ten trips for gruel and bones. Clan of Dnogn has surplus waiting."

"What?," Abneof responds.

"Oh," the man replies. "Dnogn doesn't share business with sub-alpha Abneof? Yes, Crush House owes Dnogn lots of gruel and bones."

"Oh," Abneof responds, confused, lowering his head again.

"Gimme chain. Wait here, Abneof," the man instructs as his arm extends out of the door.

Abneof hands him the chain and steps aside.

The man pulls the five Feauviums inside the Crash House and closes the door behind him.

Abneof stands outside. He hears grunting and screaming, then quiet.

The door opens and a hand extends holding the chain. Abneof grabs it and slings it over his shoulder. The door opens wider and a barrel of gruel is placed in front of him by the man who took the five Fauviums inside.

"Here is your gruel," the man states. "You know where to get the bones. Ha ha ha."

The man returns to the Crush House and closes the door behind him.

Abneof looks down at the barrel, then over to the pile of bones.

He picks up the barrel and struggles to place it over his shoulder.

He walks over to the pile of bones. He places the barrel down and takes the chains off of his shoulder, laying them flat on the ground.

Abneof meticulously places bone after bone in a pile on the center of the chains. Struggling with exhaustion, Abneof tries to hurry so that he can get back to clan Dnogn to complete his other chores.

When Abneof is done piling the bones onto the chains, he wraps them and locks the chains together. He bends over, picks up the barrel and places it over his shoulder.

Abneof picks up the end of the chain and pulls the bones behind him as he walks back in the direction of clan Dnogn.

Chapter 14

It is mid afternoon as Abneof returns to clan Dnogn. As he walks up on the fire pit, he sees Dnogn laying back on a rock napping. Dnogn hears him coming and sits up. As Abneof nears Dnogn, Dnogn shakes his head and stands.

Abneof places the barrel of gruel at the edge of the fire pit. He pulls the chains to the side of the fire pit and unlocks the chains. He places the bones in a pile and removes the chains.

Abneof stands. He turns to see Dnogn in front of him.

Dnogn smacks Abneof with a nasty right hook, knocking him off balance.

Abneof angrily stands and postures for a fight.

"Go ahead," Dnogn angrily states. "I know you want to hit me back. DO IT!"

Abneof shutters at Dnogn's anger and lowers his head in submission.

"You fool, Abneof," Dnogn begins, "one of the cages was unlocked and we lost over half of the little ones."

Abneof looks up, shocked and stutters, "What? How? I.. I... "

"STOP," Dnogn yells. "You fool! No more flesh for you. You stayed up all night with the women and got sloppy. Dnogn suffered. Look what the little ones did to Dnogn."

Abneoff looks at the cuts and bruises on Dnogn and apologizes, "I'm sorry, Dnogn. Won't happen again."

"I know it won't," Dnogn exclaims. "Take the gruel to the Holding Barn, clean it up and then feed everyone. AND, no touchin' the women. You get no flesh now. Understand?"

"Yes, Dnogn," Abneof replies submissively as he turns around and walks towards the barrel of gruel, defeated.

Abneof pics up the barrel and places it over his shoulder.

Dnogn returns to the rock he was at and lays back down.

Abneof sluggishly walks to the Holding Barn.

Chapter 15

"Poor little ones," Abneof talks to the young boys of clan Dnogn as he is cleaning the holdng barn. "Abneof is sorry he failed you. Abneof was tired from flesh this morning. You should have never ran. But, you don't know. These walls are all you've ever known."

Abneof continues to feed the little ones, being extra careful to lock each cage after he places the bowls of gruel inside. When he comes across an injured little one, he looks at the wound and pats it on the head.

The little ones are tired and whimpering. After seeing the reality of Feauvium, they are defeated and more accepting of their place in the Holding Barn.

As Abneof is tending to the last cage, Dnogn opens the door and walks into the Holding Barn.

"Are you done yet, Abneof?," Dnogn asks.

"No," Abneof responds. "I still have to collect the bowls. The boys are done eating. We lost a lot of them today."

"I know we did, you fool," Dnogn responds. "What is the count?"

"We only have a third left from this morning, Dnogn," Abneof quietly responds, scared of Dnogn's reaction.

"WHAT?," Dnogn yells. "That is worst than I thought. It's going to take years to make it up."

Dnogn walks over to Abneof and smacks him with a left cross. Abneof tumbles to the ground. The little ones begin to get agitated and howl.

"STOP!" Dnogn yells. "Get up, fool. Find me a nice juicy boy to eat. I'm hungry."

Abneof gets up and stammers to a cage with an injured young boy. He opens the cage, reaches in, grabs the boy, pulls him out and then locks the cage back up.

He stands and walks over to Dnogn, holding the little one by the feet. With his head lowered, he hands the boy to Dnogn.

Dnogn takes the boy and immediately cracks his kneck. The boy falls limp in his hands.

"This one looks tasty, yum," Dnogn states as he places the boys hand in his mouth and bites down, ripping the hand from the arm.

Dnogn crunches as he chews the hand. He swallows then bites off the other hand. He stands there, eating the boy in front of Abneof.

"Abneof hungry too," Abneof exclaims.

"Too bad, fool," Dnogn declares. "Gruel for you tonight."

Abneof looks at Dnogn shocked and says, "Abneof always gets boy."

"Not tonight, fool," Dnogn declares. "Your boys got eaten by Crackel. You get no more for long time, fool."

Abneof growls.

"WHAT?," Dnogn yells, raising the back of his hand to Abneof. "Maybe you want a hit from Dnogn again."

"No, Dnogn," Abneof retains his submissive posture. "Abneof understands. Abneof eats gruel."

"Good," Dnogn states as he takes a bite of the foot and chews it up.

Swallowing, Dnogn demands, "Get another boy. Dnogn eats with Xechia tonight by the fire."

"Yes, Dnogn. Abneof understands. I'll get a nice boy for you and Xechia."

Abneof turns and heads towards the cages to fulfill Dnogn's request.

Chapter 16

Dnogn and Xechia are sitting on rocks at the fire pit. The fire is blazing. They are eating and having a good time. Dnogn is biting off pieces of a little one and feeding Xechia.

"Here my little woman, eat the boy," Dnogn says as he feeds Xechia. "Woman must be strong to make more tasty boys."

Xechia accepts the piece of boy from Dnogn and smiles as she chews. She moves closer to Dnogn and starts to touch him.

Dnogn continues to feed Xecha.

The fire begins to go down.

Dnogn stands up and hands the remainder of the boy to Xechia.

"Dnogn got to get more bones on the fire," he says walking to the pile of bones. "Dnogn wants flesh of woman by fire tonight. Got to make it nice and burnin'."

Dnogn walks to the pile of bones and grabs an arm full. He turns to fire and throws them on. The fire blazes as he returns to Xechia sitting on the rock.

"Come to Dnogn, woman," he commands.

Xenia, taking the last bite of boy, wipes her mouth and moves closer to Dnogn. Dnogn lays back. Xechia climbs on top of him.

"Yes," Dnogn says. "Dnogn gives woman seed."

Xechia is on top of Dnogn, riding him furiously. Dnogn is pulling and tugging on her. They are both grinding into each other.

Suddenly, Dnogn gasps.

Xechia feels Dnogn's lifeless body, opens her eyes and looks up. Horrified, she sees Abneof standing over Dnogn with long bone in his hands. The other end is impaled in Dnogn's bloody skull.

"I AM DNOGN," the former Abneof yells, lifting his hands in victory. "I AM DNOGN!"

The new Dnogn starts cackling and dancing around the fire.

Xechia, still in shock, continues to sit upon the dead Feauvium beneath her. She begins to pet his head, rubbing his blood over his face and chest.

"Up, woman," Dnogn commands as he grabs Xechia's arm, pulling her off the lifeless body. "This one is burnin'."

As the new Dnogn throws Xechia to the ground, he grabs the lifeless body of the former Dnogn and lifts it over his head.

"I AM DNOGN," he declares, throwing the body into the blazing fire.

The new Dnogn begins to dance around the fire.

Xechia watches as she gets back on the rock and sits.

The new Dnogn stops, looks in the direction of Xechia and yells, "I AM DNOGN!"

He composes himself and walks towards Xechia.

Xechia cowls as Dnogn approaches.

He grabs her by the arm and pulls her off the rock.

"Come, woman," Dnogn exclaims. "Dnogn hungry. Dnogn wants taste of little girl. Dnogn wants flesh all night."

Dnogn pulls Xechia next to him as he walks in the direction of the Brood House.

"I AM DNOGN," Dnogn exclaims as he walks into the darkness.

Chapter 17

The women of the Brood House are prepping and preparing for Dnogn. They are in the big, main room of the house, laughing and talking.

As the door opens, the women turn to see Xechia thrown to the floor in front of them. She remains kneeling before them as Dnogn walks in.

Dnongn walks in and stands just in the room. He stands tall. He pauses for a moment, looking over the women in the Brood House who are trying to figure out what is going on.

"I AM DNOGN," Dnogn exclaims loudly raising his arms and head in triumph.

The women of the Brood House look at each other, smile and begin to cheer.

Xechia stands, walks over to Dnogn and jumps on him.

The other women of the Brood House surround him and start to pet him.

They pick him up and take him back to the Dnogn bed and proceed to take his seed.

About the Author

Mark F. Kalita is the author of over 40 books on Spirituality and our Spiritual nature. Mark believes that it is his purpose in life to transfer this knowledge of the Ascensions and the Light of the Angelic Realm to our People.

Besides his role as Author, Mark also teaches workshops such as the "Ascension Workshop". With interests in Tarot, Crystals, Healing and other Spiritual Gifts, Mark wants to share his knowledge with others.

When Mark isn't writing or teaching, he spends time outdoors planting or planning gardens. His vision is to create a vast wilderness of food to provide sustenance for our People. From fruit bearing trees to herbs and edibles, Mark's dream is to create a new epoch of lovingkindness in which all of our basic needs are met – beginning with food!

Each new story Mark creates is an inspirational bridge to a world that could be. A world without suffering. A world bathed in the Light of knowledge and compassion founded in the Unity of Existence.

Other books by
Mark F. Kalita

These and other books can all be found at:

www.KALITA.com

Or, through Amazon in paperback or Kindle

"Dance of the Blue Star Kachina" A short story based on Hopi legend. Read how the mystical dance of an ancient priest opens up a world of spirit and brings his brother back to destroy the modern world.

"Jesus Fallacy" was the first science fiction short story by Mark F. Kalita. It is the story of the Archangel Mika'el, from a planet of Light, as he descends to the Earth, living many Incarnations while teaching about Light and Darkness.

"Matrix of ONE: Winning the Game of Life" looks at the nature of existence through the eyes of a game analogy. The ONE, Path of Being and our Avatars are discussed along with the path of Light.

"Tellurian" is short story that serves as a manual for inhabitants of the earth to explain the Heavens and our Spiritual foundations so that we may live in peace, truth and altruistic lovingkindness for evermore.

Discover Mark F. Kalita's
Science Fiction Series

"ASCENSION STAGE"

The "Ascension Stage" series of cross genre science fiction short stories is based on the short story "Jesus Fallacy" by Mark F. Kalita. Each short story visits a different world in our journey back to the ONE.

"Jesus Fallacy" is the story of Archangel Mika'el and his journey through the Realm of Earth. On his journey, through multiple Incarnations, he experiences Love and Purpose, teaching the Light and Dark Angels of lower Octaves.

Join Mika'el and his army of Angels as they journey through the "Jesus Fallacy" and prepare the Realm of the Earth for the Ascension of All.

www.AscensionStage.com

or follow the adventures at

Twitter @AscensionStages

www.ingramcontent.com/pod-product-compliance
Lightning Source LLC
Chambersburg PA
CBHW051010050726
47592CB00007B/2787